To the Pryor mob, my family: Dad, Monty Senior; Mum, Dot; my seven sisters, Sue, Cilla, Chrissy, Kim, Lynette, Toni and Adrena; and my three brothers, Nick, Roscoe and Paul. I thank you all and I love you all.

B.M.P.

For my son, Cody.

R.S.

To listen to Boori reading this book in Kunggandji and English,

please scan the QR code, or go to www.allenandunwin.com/story-doctors

STORY DOCTORS

BOORI MONTY PRYOR

ILLUSTRATED BY RITA SINCLAIR

ALLEN&UNWIN
SYDNEY • MELBOURNE • AUCKLAND • LONDON

From whence we came
the sum of some
observed the tracks from where we'd come.

Heel and toe, tread heat and snow.
Impressions left behind
of footprints so maligned.

Standing tall, writes on the wall,
with spit and ochre, charcoal too.
All this written just for you.

From foot through hand, a nurtured land
speaks through charcoal beings.

What lies within
can now begin,
across cathedral walls.
This stony face, a storied place.

Where animals animate,
and beings gravitate,
to do a dance entwined,
in charcoal so refined.

Spit and ochre, they talk too,
that's nothing new,
with lore and order.
It's life's recorder.

KING

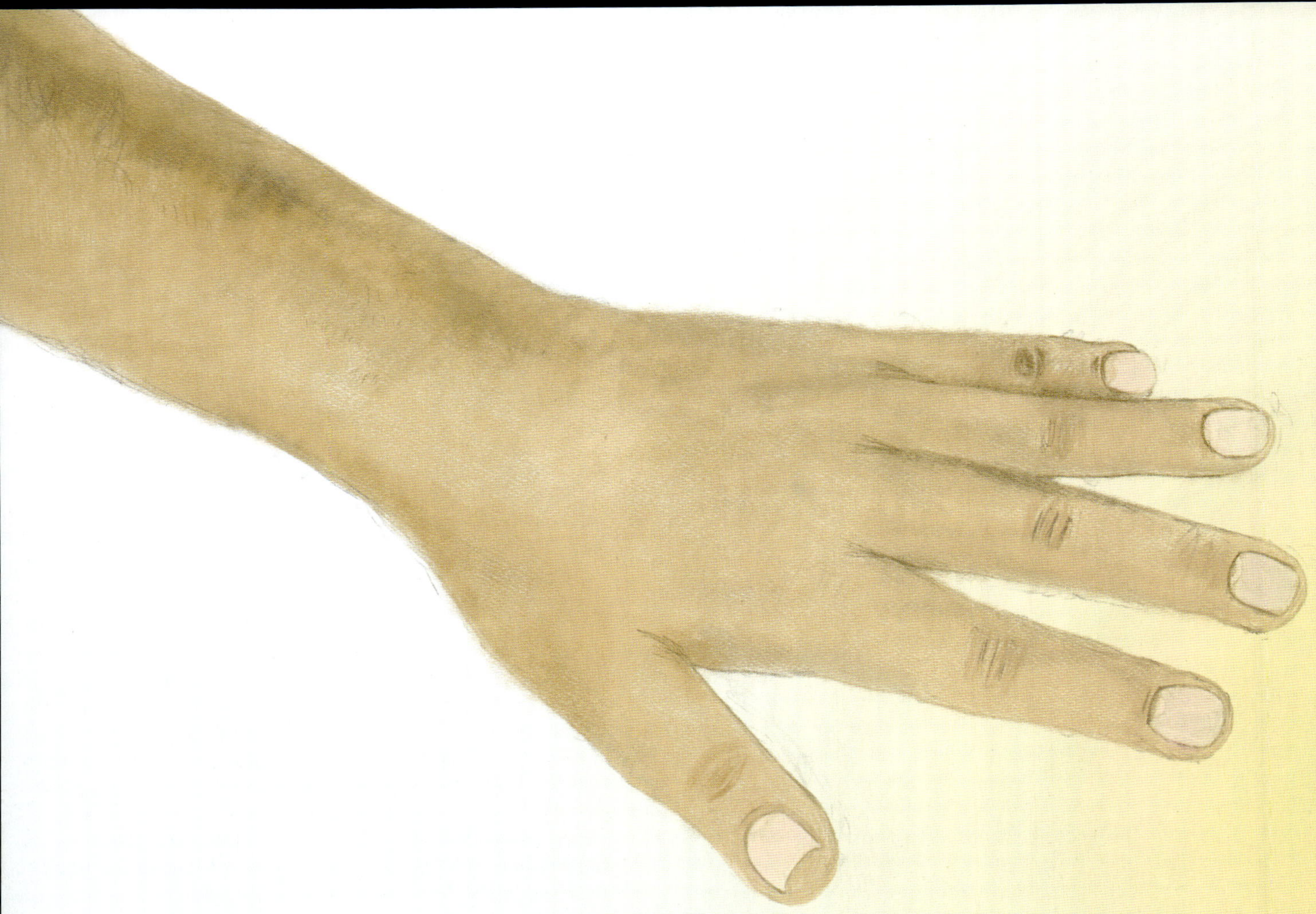

So...this new way of learning,
is it really so concerning?

If you try, you will spy
the reason there's no treason.
It belies your sighs.
Just drink the stories through your eyes.

Hands’ ochre prints are earthy hints,
connecting then to now,
so past can then avow.

This new-age healing, that inner feeling,
two centuries to cure,
of belongings insecure.

The pharmacies abound,
above and underground,
green shoots so small, to trees so tall.

Helps breathe in all our glories,
the medicines in our stories.
That stony face, our storied place.

The prescriptions are sublime, and written over time.
Doctor's orders, there are no borders.

When it comes to we as one,
belonging's said and done,
so, self-medicate, then meditate.

As cathedrals echo time,
and footprints' rhythm steps the rhyme,
prescriptions so sublime.

Our future is the past.
Will learning from it last?
Elementary is the focus,
there is no hocus-pocus.

Be that tall being, and animals that you're seeing.
Dance among the dust.
In us the dust we trust.

From whence we came,
the sum of some,
from where we come.
impressions left
SOVEREIGNTY
ABORIGINAL EMBASSY
prints so maligned. Standing tall, writes
ochre, charcoal too, all this
behind,
on the wall
foot through hand,
charcoal beings. What lies
land, speaks
FLOUR
Sunshine milk
CORNED BEEF
across cathedral walls, this
animals animate,
TERRA NULLIUS
stony face,
gravitate to do a dance
so refined.
NO PRIDE IN GENOCIDE
NO ROOM FOR RACISM
STOLEN WAGES...
STOLEN GENERATIONS
STOLEN LAND...
VOTE YES FOR ABORIGINAL RIGHTS
STOP INDIGENOUS DEATHS IN CUSTODY
too, thats nothing new,
life recorder
of learning, is it really
try, you will
no treason, it belies your
stories
STEEDEN
SHERRIN
1868
PERMISSION TO TRAVEL

Soft earth, soft feet,
feel the beat,
that lovely earthy sound,
sinking in the ground.

Nature nurtures roots anew.
The harshness of this land is true.
Through roots of old, truth be told.

Through movie tones, and pigment bones,
its tune is played, long life displayed.

Now all of us, we dance in dust,
harsh but honour-bound,
to dance this new-found sound.

Green shoots so small,
to trees so tall.

Breathe,
believe.
It's in the song…

OUR
STORY

…if we listen, we all belong.

Eco Echoes
Words of Medicine

Somewhere in the midst of 2018, I had this feeling that one day very soon, our country, Australia, was going to get very sick. We as a nation have been unwell for a very long time now, and I myself was sick of being sick, and felt that what we all needed was a different kind of medicine. The kind that should have been taken well before those annoying symptoms raised their ugly heads.

The medicine I'm talking about is a very special kind of medicine. And it can only be found in one place. It's right there in those eco echoes – the ones that have travelled through the voices from the oldest continuous living culture in the world.

Australia is made up of thirty per cent desert, and is the driest continent in the world. First Nations people were shaped from and by the earth. We know each other very well – so much so that we define longevity and defy logic.

So, this got me thinking, could there be any way possible to take these eco echoes, and shape their wise voices into written words of medicine?

Fear, anger, self-loathing, loss of worth and guilt punctured my heart again. I cried, I sobbed, I yelled, I screamed, I was in so much pain that

I felt I couldn't stop the bleeding. Because I knew that if I had any chance at all to have these written words listen to those eco echoes, I'd have to wrestle with these monsters once again.

As I began to write, there in my small room in Carlton, Melbourne, these monsters surrounded me, looking for a fight. I wrestled and fought to pick my words carefully, denying them any chance to poison my thoughts.

Then, two lines in one month, my heart stopped bleeding. Five lines in two months, bandaids appeared. Ten lines in three months, the pain still lingered. Then, six lines in one month, I was breathing with no pain in my heart.

My heart was happy. Because these eco echoes and those written words have finally met, and like each other. So now they have gotten together and shaped these wise voices into written words of medicine.

Hopefully, when you read these words, unknowingly, you will taste that medicine. I fought so very hard to find a way to heal – I really gave it my best shot. I hope you find yourself, alive and well, within the covers of this book.

Boori Monty Pryor

BOORI MONTY PRYOR was born in Townsville, North Queensland. His father is from the Juru people of Cape Upstart from the Bowen region. His mother is a descendant of the Gurubana Moiety group from the Kunggandji Nation near Cairns. Boori is a multi-talented performer who has worked in film and television (as an actor and writer), modelling, sport, music and theatre-in-education. Boori has written several award-winning children's books, including Prime Minister's Literary Award winner *Shake a Leg*, and was Australia's inaugural Children's Laureate (with Alison Lester) in 2012 and 2013. He co-wrote and is the subject of *Wrong Kind of Black* (International Emmy Award nominee, screening on Netflix) and *Brown Paper Bag* (in which he also stars), and during his career as a storyteller he has worked with over one million children.

RITA SINCLAIR was born in Mareeba, North Queensland, and grew up a bit further south, in Townsville. As a child, she spent a lot of time daydreaming, drawing and reading, often in a tree or under its branches. Rita blames her mum for her love of all books (especially picture books), because books were a part of every birthday or Christmas. When her son, Cody, was born, Rita was excited to have a reason to buy more books. Now that he is grown up and married, she buys picture books for herself, just because. Rita has worked as an ice-cream and snack bar attendant, greyhound race photographer, wedding videographer, stained-glass overlay operator, teacher, librarian, wedding celebrant and now illustrator. She believes in lifelong learning and is always ready to learn something new – she often has several random courses lined up, and there is always a stack or two of books waiting for the holidays to be read.

First published by Allen & Unwin in 2021

The illustrator claims no ownership over any First Nations cultural material referenced in the story.

Allen & Unwin
83 Alexander Street
Crows Nest NSW 2065
Australia
Phone: (61 2) 8425 0100
Email: info@allenandunwin.com
Web: www.allenandunwin.com

NATIONAL LIBRARY OF AUSTRALIA
A catalogue record for this book is available from the National Library of Australia

ISBN 978 1 76052 655 9

For teaching resources, explore www.allenandunwin.com/resources/for-teachers

Illustration technique: hand-drawn with Apple Pencil on iPad Air using Procreate

Cover and text design by Sandra Nobes
Illustration on page 21 is partially based on photographs of Boori's family, with permission
Set in 20 pt Sofia Pro by Sandra Nobes
This book was printed in March 2025 by Hang Tai Printing Company Limited, China

5 7 9 10 8 6

FSC www.fsc.org MIX Paper | Supporting responsible forestry FSC® C023121

www.facebook.com/boorimontypryor